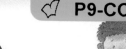

Mm

Ll

Gg Hh Ii Jj Kk

Uu Vv Ww Xx Yy Zz

Dear Parent,

The My First Steps to Reading® *series is based on a teaching activity that helps children learn to recognize letters and their sounds. The use of predictable language patterns and repetition of familiar words will also help your child build a basic sight vocabulary. Your child will enjoy watching the characters in the books place imaginative objects in "letter boxes." You and your child can even create and fill your own letter box, using stuffed animals, cut-out pictures, or other objects beginning with the same letter. The things you can do together are limited only by your imagination. Learning letters will be fun—the first important step on the road to reading.*

The Editors

All Rights Reserved. Published by Scholastic Inc., 90 Old Sherman Turnpike, Danbury, Connecticut 06810, by arrangement with The Child's World, Inc.
Scholastic offers a varied selection of children's book racks and tote bags. For details about ordering, please write to: Scholastic At Home, 90 Old Sherman Turnpike, Danbury, CT 06810, Attention: Premium Department

Originally published as *My "u" Sound Box* by The Child's World, Inc.

My First Steps to Reading is a registered trademark of Grolier Publishing Co. Inc.
SCHOLASTIC and associated logos are trademarks and/or registered trademarks of Scholastic Inc.

Printed in the U.S.A.

My "u" Book

(This book concentrates on the short "u" sound in the story line.
Words beginning with the long "u" sound are included
at the end of the book.)

written by Jane Belk Moncure
illustrated by Colin King

Little  had a box.

"I will find things that begin
with my 'u' sound," she said.

"I will put them into my sound box."

"First I will find an umbrella."

"I will run, run, run

to find an umbrella."

Why did Little  get under the box?

Why was the box upside down?

Little u found an umbrella.

She found lots of umbrellas.

She put one umbrella over her head.
Did she put the other umbrellas

into her box?

She did.

Just then, the sun came out.

Little U put the umbrella down.

But then the rain came down again.

Little u put the umbrella up.

Then she saw some underclothes.

They were getting wet.

She took the underclothes off the line.

She put them into her box.

Little  u took the underclothes upstairs.

She put the underclothes away.

"Now," she said, "I can play under my umbrella."

She went out in the rain.

"I can run through a

puddle,"

she said. "What fun!"

Then Little  found an ugly duckling.

The ugly duckling was grumpy.

She put the ugly duckling into her box.

"Do not be grumpy," she said.
"You will grow up to be pretty."

Just then, she saw her uncle.

He was getting wet, so

Little  gave her uncle

an umbrella.

Next, she saw an umpire.

"Can you help us?" he asked.

"We are playing a game in the rain.

We need umbrellas."

Little  u said, "I have a box full
of umbrellas."

She gave the umpire an umbrella.

Then she gave everyone an umbrella.

underclothes

ugly
duckling

umbrella

umpire

uncle

What fun they had in the rain.

Can you read these words

with Little 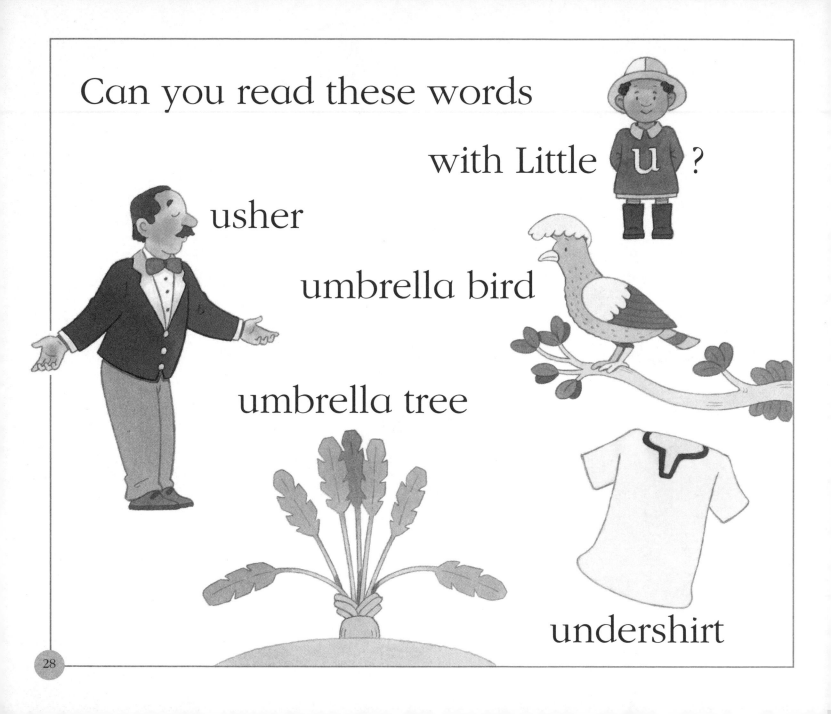 ?

usher

umbrella bird

umbrella tree

undershirt

Little 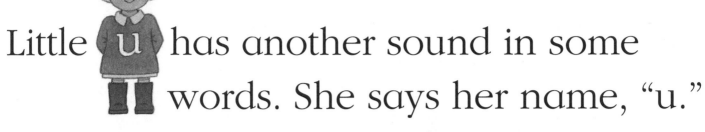 has another sound in some words. She says her name, "u."

Can you read these words? Listen for Little 's name.

ukulele

unicorn

uniform

Aa Bb Cc Dd Ee Ff

Nn Oo Pp Qq Rr Ss Tt

My First Steps to READING®